SKY

PAMELA PORTER

•

WITH PICTURES BY
Mary Jane Gerber

A GROUNDWOOD BOOK
HOUSE OF ANANSI PRESS
TORONTO BERKELEY

Groundwood Books /House of Anansi Press
110 Spadina Avenue, Suite 801, Toronto, Ontario M5V 2K4
Distributed in the USA by Publishers Group West
1700 Fourth Street, Berkeley, CA 94710

We acknowledge for their financial support of our publishing program
the Canada Council for the Arts, the Government of Canada through
the Book Publishing Industry Development Program (BPIDP), the
Ontario Arts Council and the Government of Ontario through the
Ontario Media Development Corporation's Ontario Book Initiative.

ONTARIO ARTS COUNCIL
CONSEIL DES ARTS DE L'ONTARIO

National Library of Canada Cataloging in Publication
Porter, Pamela Paige
Sky / by Pamela Porter; illustrated by Mary Jane Gerber.
ISBN 0-88899-563-6 (bound).–ISBN 0-88899-607-1 (pbk.)
1. Métis–Juvenile fiction. 2. Blackfeet Indian Reservation
(Mont.)–Juvenile fiction. 3. Horses–Juvenile fiction.
I. Gerber, Mary Jane II. Title.
PS8581.O7573S59 2004   jC813'.6   C2004-902839-1

Design by Michael Solomon

For Georgia, who lived it.

1

THERE'D BEEN more snow than I'd ever seen that winter. Some days I had to miss school because Paw Paw's old car was just buried in snow, and there was no way we could get out to the road where the school bus stopped until Buzz, our neighbor, climbed into his grader and plowed us out.

We birthed lots of lambs that year – I think about thirty – and about twenty-five of them survived, which is an amazing number when you think about lambs, because new-born lambs are hard to keep alive sometimes. They'll get born and go along just fine. Then one of them will fall over and die. And that winter, with all the snow, I guess it was good some of the time that I couldn't get to school, because Paw Paw needed my help with the lambing.

We'd have to plow through the snow on foot with me, Georgia Salois, trying to match my age-eleven feet with Paw Paw's I-don't-know-how-old feet making tracks knee deep in the snow toward the barn in the dark. We'd go out there just before my bedtime to see if any of the female sheep looked about to give birth. And if one of them was about to, or was lying in the straw breathing hard or making sick-sounding noises, then Paw Paw and I had to stay there until it was born.

A lot of times it taken most of the night and all my energy just to stay somewhat warm out there when it was about twenty below outside the barn, and not much warmer inside. Lambs have this way of getting born in the coldest part of the winter, and our lambs were no exception.

When one of the lambs finally come out of its mom, usually at about three in the morning, it'd slide out all slimy, and Paw Paw and I would quick wipe the slime off its nose so it could get a breath. Then the mother would lick the rest of the gunk off of it, and the baby would slowly start to look like a living animal, so white and pink it made the snow look dull. We'd try to have the baby suck milk from its mom, and when it got some, we'd wrap it in a blanket and rush up to the house, where it would spend the rest of the night in front of our kitchen stove. Then Gramma would wake up and brush its white wool all fluffy, so that by morning, when everything was done and we had a new lamb, I was too drag-down tired to go to school, even if the snow wouldn't have kept me home.

When the snow melted that year, it just kept on raining and raining. Birch Creek rushed brown and high beside our cabin, and our sheep wouldn't leave the barn. Of course, then the lambs wouldn't go out either. Gramma kept saying that with all the births we'd be out of debt by August, but then they couldn't get out to grass. So we had to bring some of last year's hay in to them. Even with that, a couple of the youngest lambs fallen over and died.

That's about the way things were when it happened.

2

I CAN HARDLY remember a time when I didn't live with Gramma and Paw Paw high in the scrub pines on the edge of the Blackfeet Reservation in northern Montana. I've got the soil of that place scrubbed into my skin, the wind blown fresh and cold into my lungs. I've got the piney smell from the mountains behind us in my hair.

People say it's a rough land, that it's claimed a lot of lives. It almost claimed me.

Gramma says I'm a survivor, because my mom, my dad, my little brother and I were all in the same car when it skidded over the cliff, and I was the only one to survive. That happened in early spring, too, just about lambing season. My dad was about to go off and join the navy over at Bremerton, Washington, the very next day. Everybody was real proud of him for getting into the navy. It was supposed to be a good job.

We were coming back from having supper with Gramma and Paw Paw when the car my dad was driving started sliding on black ice on a curve around a big hill, and the car flown off the road and straight down the side of the hill. Gramma never liked to talk about it, but once she did say that I was thrown out of the car and ended up in a tree. That's how come I lived and everyone else didn't.

They buried my mom, my dad and my brother here, not far from Gramma and Paw Paw's house.

The scar above my eye is from that accident. My left eyebrow never grew back quite right after the doctor took the stitches out, and some of it's still missing.

Sometimes I still try to remember what they looked like. Whenever we had to drive on that piece of road, I used to squeeze my eyes shut and hang on tight to something inside the car, thinking I was going to fly off again. I don't know what Gramma and Paw Paw thought at those times, because they always stopped talking when we got to that curve, and then they'd be silent all the rest of the way home. And I'd be alone in the back seat breaking out in a sweat.

That spring after the lambs were born, we'd slog out in the fat snow and rain and mud to watch Birch Creek rise a little more – Paw Paw, Gramma and me. And sometimes my Uncle Lester would come along and wonder out loud about how the dam was holding up.

"They sure is letting a ton a water off that dam," my uncle would say, staring away into the mountains.

Paw Paw would nod or say something low and grumbling in the old language.

Gramma and I, we always read the newspaper together, and we seen the story about the water company assuring folks that the dam would hold. It said they sent letters out to everybody downstream to calm them.

Gramma said, "We live downstream sure as anybody and we didn't get no letter."

I knew we hadn't gotten a letter because I always brought the mail up to the house when I come home from school.

My uncle said, "Ain't got no letter from nobody."

Gramma and I checked around. None of the Indian people we'd talked to got any letter from the water company.

Nights I'd lie on my mattress listening to Paw Paw snore and Birch Creek roar. I hoped the dam wouldn't bust with all of us asleep. Sometimes I'd be too scared to sleep, listening for some sound or other… And I broken out in a sweat just waiting for something to happen, wondering what I'd do first, second and third if the dam really busted out.

3

BUT IT WAS an afternoon when it happened. I gone to the back windowsill to get Paw Paw's carving knife for him, and I seen it even before I could hear it.

"Paw Paw! Gramma! It's broke! It's broke!"

Out of that spot where our quiet creek had always just skipped off the mountains, that place my uncle had stared into only a day or so before, I seen a wall of water tall as the mountain itself.

And I knew.

I yelled at them. They seemed to sit still forever. Finally Paw Paw and I started grabbing everything we could − blankets off the bed, a pillow or two, a loaf of bread, our water basin. We thrown them into the car. Gramma was puttering around looking for I didn't know what.

Already the water was so loud we had to yell to be heard.

"C'mon, Gramma, we gotta get to the car!"

I tried to drag her to the door. Then I seen Gramma and Paw Paw's picture album. I grabbed it and ran outside. Gramma was fumbling with her keys, trying to lock the door.

"We don't have time, Gramma!" I yelled over the water coming, pulling her toward the car. There wasn't going to be nothing left to lock.

Water from the creek began to lap around our shoes as I helped Gramma into the car Paw Paw had running. The car squealed as Paw Paw turned it around and out the yard.

Then it come.

I turned around and it was behind us. The wall lifted our car up and thrown us

aside like a big rock. I don't know how we landed back on the ground out of the path of the water wall, and I don't know how Paw Paw just kept on driving, but he did.

When I turned back again, everything was gone – our house, the barn, everything.

I checked our little pile of belongings. We had no clothes but what we were wearing, a wash basin, a few blankets.

Then my heart stopped.

Daisy, my stuffed horse. I'd won her at the State Fair. She was the only stuffed animal I'd ever owned, and I'd left her behind.

I couldn't stop the tears that came then.

I guess Gramma heard me back there crying, because she reached her hand over the seat. I held it tight and we rode up the hill, around the famous curve and quietly into town.

4

PAW PAW DROVE around town, I think wondering what to do. Driving around town didn't take a lot of time, but Paw Paw driven real slow. When we come up to the high school, we seen people going in there. Turned out the gym was being set up as a place where folks who'd lost their homes could go.

Paw Paw turned the car into the school parking lot. The sheriff, Bill Smiley, was standing by the door to the gym. Almost before we could get out of the car, he walked up to us.

Sheriff Smiley seen Paw Paw's long braids.

"Gym's full," he told Paw Paw. He had us follow him to a classroom where a whole lot of Indians were crushed together with whatever they managed to save, like us.

Desks and chairs had been shoved to one side. Some little kids were drawing with chalk on the blackboards. Cards showing how to write the alphabet hung above the board at one end of the room.

The whole place smelled like damp mixed with smoke. Like clothes and blankets and people that got wet. Clothes and blankets and people that smelled like smoke from the stoves in their houses that got carried off by the water.

Some people were quietly asking if anyone had seen their relatives. Others asked about their neighbors. People were glad to see us when we walked in.

Gramma looked around and said to the hushed room, "Lester? Buzz?" A couple of the elders shook their heads.

We're the lucky ones, being here, I told myself, but I didn't know how we were all going to sleep at night. There wasn't enough room for everyone to lie down.

We sagged onto the floor, not saying a word, for it seemed like forever. I looked out the windows at the darkening sky and realized it must be getting night.

I tugged at Paw Paw's sleeve and whispered, "What time's it coming up on?"

Paw Paw checked his watch. "Near nine o'clock, if my watch is still working."

We sat until we could barely see each other. Then the sheriff walked in and turned on the light. We squinted and blinked up at him.

"Okay, you can eat now. Five dollars per family."

Some of the people didn't have nothing for money.

"How much you got, Paw Paw? Gramma?" I whispered.

Paw Paw looked in his wallet. Twenty-five dollars. Gramma clutched her change purse tight. I helped her open it and we counted the money. Nine dollars and forty-three cents.

Paw Paw given five dollars to Jenny

Yellowrobe's mom so they could eat. He given five dollars to Sheriff Smiley so we could eat. After that I figured we had twenty-four dollars and forty-three cents total.

I scooted over toward Jenny, my best friend in school. On her lap sat Carla, her baby sister. Jenny had two older brothers and a younger brother and sister, and her mom. Me and Jenny made up the fifth grade at our school of seven kids, most of them Yellowrobes.

"Your house gone?" I whispered to Jenny. She nodded. "Yours?"

I nodded. I couldn't speak the words for what happened. "What're you gonna do?"

"Stay here, I guess," Jenny said, "Till we find some other place to live. They said they'll be operating this three or four nights."

Jenny took one of Carla's hands and I took the other as we stood up. The sheriff led us into the gym where the people who weren't Indian were lying on cots with pillows and blankets on them. A few people were picking up plates and forks and knives from the long tables on one side of the gym where people had eaten. We waited in line for the ladies to slop some food onto plates for us.

The lady holding the fresh plates said, "Y'all know there's charge for the plates and utensils. Dollar a set."

That was three dollars for us. Six dollars for the Yellowrobes.

After that I figured we had fifteen dollars and forty-three cents left.

After we sat down to eat, a family was brought in and shown to some cots. There was a dad and mom and three red-haired, freckle-faced kids – all boys who looked so much alike they could have been three different sizes of the same kid. That family walked past us to the eating place.

"How much all this gonna cost?" the man asked the same lady who'd held our plates.

"It's free, sir," she said. "All you can eat."

None of us at the Indian table even tried going back for seconds.

My stomach was tied up so tight I could barely eat anyway, and Gramma just pushed the food around with her fork mostly. When we finished we given all the plates and forks and spoons back to the servers and shuffled off to our room still hot from all the people.

The grownups sat up all night so us kids could lie down. We put the blankets under us for softness from the cold linoleum floor, Gramma and Paw Paw sharing one blanket and me lying on the other. I told Gramma she should take our pillows to cushion her back gone bad from all those years of lambing and chopping wood and stoking the stove. Gramma said I should take one pillow. Paw Paw didn't have nothing for a pillow.

As soon as my face hit that pillow it was wet with tears. I wasn't crying so much for our house or even for the lambs that I'd fussed over so much. I was crying for my Daisy that I'd left behind, because she was supposed to be the second thing I saved after Gramma and Paw Paw, and because there

wasn't any spot on this earth that we belonged to anymore.

And because nobody knew where Uncle Lester was, or Buzz.

5

MORNING WOKE me with sun streaming right into my face. Paw Paw sat propped against the wall, snoring. Two men picked their way over the sleeping bodies toward us. I rubbed my eyes and squinted.

"Buzz! Uncle Lester!" I nearly shouted, waking Gramma and Paw Paw and causing little Carla Yellowrobe to stir nearby.

"Hey, Georgia, little lady," Uncle Lester said grinning. His missing teeth always made his mouth look like one of those picket fences in front of the houses in town.

The four grownups broke into the old language that I didn't much speak, though I understood it. Buzz's house was gone, too.

He'd slept in his truck overnight. He didn't want to come here. He knew they'd make the Indians bow down for everything, he said. And even though he wasn't Indian by blood, he was Indian in spirit, and he couldn't sleep out there in a cot with all of us cramped in this room.

Uncle Lester hadn't got hit by the flood. He come looking for us here and found Buzz sleeping in his truck.

I remembered something. Uncle Lester had an extra room in his house. I didn't like the idea of sleeping and eating here another night. Besides, we couldn't afford it. And if Gramma and Paw Paw weren't going to bring up the subject of Lester's extra room, I was.

"We have to come stay in your spare room," I said flatly.

"I got lots of people want to stay in my spare room. What you gonna give me for my trouble?"

He didn't look at me but at Paw Paw's belt buckle, the silver one with a real star sapphire in it. Paw Paw won it at the 1922 Indian Rodeo. Grand prize. Paw Paw could still rope a sheep or calf from a moving horse better than anyone.

I couldn't stand the thought of Paw Paw giving it away. I'd sleep on the ground first.

"Fifteen dollars is what we got. Take it or leave it." I slid closer to Paw Paw to guard that buckle if I had to.

"You're a tough customer, little lady," said Uncle Lester, holding out an open palm.

I glanced over at Jenny Yellowrobe. She was lying there watching us pack up. With no happiness in our eyes, me and Jenny waved to each other.

By the time we'd filled our arms with blankets and pillows and walked out of that cage of a room into the free fresh air, we had forty-three cents to our name.

6

LIVING AT Uncle Lester's wasn't so bad, and he wasn't so bad, even with his trying for Paw Paw's buckle and taking the last of our money. Neighbors brought clothes for us, though nobody had much to spare, and they sent food over. Gramma done all the cooking, so Lester had it pretty good in my opinion.

Paw Paw was all different after the dam broke. He'd sit by the stove and carve a little, but he never gone out much.

None of us opened the picture album. We didn't want to look at the way things used to be.

Then something happened that brought a little of the light back into Paw Paw, and some back into me, too.

Me and Paw Paw driven out to our land to see if there was anything worth saving after the wall of water gone through. We walked all over, checking the damage.

I loved being back on our wide land. I could smell in the air the same cold, piney smell that I always remembered, but everything else was different. Birch Creek had made a big gash where our little stream used to flow. A tree trunk from way up in the mountains was lying where our barn used to be. About all that was still standing were some puny trees and bushes with matted grass and barbed-wire fence tangled in them.

Then I found her.

I still don't know how she survived those first days out there after the flood, but when I seen her she was curled up under some brush. She didn't even look like a live thing. Some fencing wire was caught all in her back legs and tail.

Then she lifted her head to look at me.

I run and yelled for Paw Paw. He come and helped me carry her up to the car.

"How old you figure she is, Paw Paw?" I asked, practically out of strength from hauling her.

"Well, she's a pretty decent-size foal, Georgia. Maybe two, three months. Depends on how big she was when she was born. Any younger and she'd have died by now."

But she was still small enough and weak enough to ride in the trunk of Paw Paw's big old car. He drove real slow with the trunk hood wide open, all the way up the dirt road and around the big, bald hill that Lester's house sat on.

If it would have been our house, Gramma, Paw Paw and me would have brought her in and made her a bed by the stove. But Uncle Lester might kick us all out for that, so we took her to his barn.

Paw Paw had to cut the wire away from her legs and out of her tail. Then he run his rough old hands over her legs.

"Can't find nothing broken," he said.

Next we wiped the mud off her, and we

could see she was a paint, white with black patches that went up into her mane. Then we wrapped a blanket around her. We made her a bed of straw, and Gramma rigged up a wet cloth in a pail until we could get to town for a bottle.

I sat down with her there in the barn and helped her suck on that wet cloth. She coughed and sputtered. Seemed like she'd got a bunch of water down her lungs. She had a lot of white stuff coming out her nose.

But her eyes – one brown, one blue. First thing Paw Paw said when he seen those eyes was, "Brown is for our Mother Earth. Blue is for our Father Sky." So I named her Sky, after that one blue eye.

Gramma said we might be able to get her better if she really was a survivor like me. I sat there a long time in the barn, stroking her all over, still holding the rag for her in case she wanted it. Paw Paw run his hands over the rest of her, but he didn't find nothing broken. Just a few cuts here and there. She'd cough, and her cough would shake her whole little body, and it was during one of those coughs that she lifted her head, and I noticed a bright red cut over her right eye.

I pointed it out to Paw Paw.

"She'll have a scar there for life, assuming she lives," he said.

A scar over her right eye. Me, over my left. I figured she was a survivor for sure, and we had a few things in common.

7

GRAMMA AND Paw Paw and me gone into town to Jake's Junk Store, and I rooted around in some bins till I found an old calving bottle and a nipple that wasn't too cracked up. Soon as we got home, Gramma mixed up some powdered milk, and Sky taken that bottle like she'd been dreaming about it for weeks. She grabbed the soft nipple part in her teeth, and she sucked so hard that I dropped the bottle trying to hold it for her. Once the nipple popped right off, splashing milk all over her nose and my jeans.

Gramma made up a batch of her famous cough medicine that was a mixture of honey, vinegar and lemon juice. Then I got the pleasure of trying to get that stuff in her mouth and down her throat with one of the cooking spoons from the kitchen.

At first it wasn't so hard because she was still weak. But in just a few days she started to stand up, and those wobbly little legs were strong. Then it taken more time because she knew right away what was milk and what was medicine.

Paw Paw said I couldn't force her. I'd have to earn her trust so she would look to me as the leader of her herd. I'd scratch her head and around her ears and tell her stories I knew, like the story of the Three Little Pigs. She seemed to like that one. Those ears would swivel around forward and sideways while I scratched and huffed and puffed, and eventually I could slip that spoon of medicine into the side of her mouth.

Now Lester had a mean horse, and I mean mean, according to some of the stories he told about that horse bucking him over fences and straight into tree trunks. Lester was real rough with him, too. I'd seen him yell and kick that horse in the ribs. He was huge, Lester's horse was, and he lived in that barn. I was plenty scared of him.

He didn't pay us no mind for the first little bit, but one day when I was out there shoveling out some of the manure and trying to clean the place up, he pinned his ears back flat and rushed toward Sky. Before I could think, I flew up behind him, yelling and holding that manure fork in the air, and Joe, that's what his name was, took off outside the barn and was galloping around the corral bucking and kicking.

I stood at the door of the barn holding that manure fork and looking out at him in the corral running in circles. I was nearly out of breath with fright, but I wasn't going to let him back in the barn to hurt Sky. He'd gallop around for awhile, throwing his head way up into thc air, then he'd slow down to a trot. But whenever he saw my eyes straight on his, he'd speed up again.

I come out into the ring some, and thrown my head as high up into the air as I could. I stood determined not to let him think I was afraid of him. I figured if I could tell him I was tough, too, and kept him running around until he was good and tired, then he had less chance of hurting my baby.

Unfortunately, Gramma, Paw Paw and Uncle Lester, they all gone over to somebody or other's ranch to look at a bunch of chickens Lester was thinking of buying. So I had to wear Joe out myself. I must have stood in that corral a half hour or more trying to get Joe wore down, and I started to notice what a pretty horse he actually was – dark red with a black mane and tail and black legs up to his knees.

And then that horse began to trot around with his head way low to the ground, sticking his tongue out and back in again, and pretty soon I figured he must be getting tired. So I turned away from him and back toward Sky. And when I was walking back into the barn, all of a sudden I felt this nose on my shoulder.

It was Joe. I turned around and he bowed his head down below mine. I just naturally started to rub his forehead and scratch under his forelock, and that old horse bounced his head up and down with my rubbing.

That was the day Joe first followed me everywhere, right off my right shoulder, and he followed me around every day after that. Paw Paw figured I'd got his attention as leader of the herd.

"Seems like leader of the herd's a whole lot of work," I said.

A little smile crept into Paw Paw's eyes.

8

WHEN WE STARTED going to school again, the bus didn't drop us off at our little school anymore. Me and Jenny and the others who'd made up our Birch Creek school rode to the big school in town. Me and Jenny and Clifford Old Person scrunched into extra seats in a class of eighteen fifth and sixth graders. We sat in our own row over by the windows. The white kids sat in all the other rows, and the teacher never looked at our row when she talked.

Recess was the worst, though. Me and Jenny would try and stay out of the way, but some of the big white boys liked to find us and dance around hollering and slapping their hands over their mouths. Freddy Yellowrobe, Jenny's oldest brother, was almost always in trouble because he got into fights with those boys, even though they never seemed to get punished.

Birch Creek School was declared too damaged by the flood to fix up for just seven of us, but it wasn't too damaged for Jenny's family. Those two big boys and their mom and Jenny got it cleaned up, and they moved in. Even the two little ones worked on it. I helped, too, lugging buckets of water from the pump to wash the floor after Jenny's brothers had shoveled all the mud out of it.

Meanwhile, Gramma and I were trying to think how we were going to get a house put up again.

Paw Paw pretty much sat by the stove each day until I come home and tried to pull him out of whatever far place he was in. Couple of times I pulled out the picture album, said maybe he could tell me a story about one of the old pictures the way he used to, but he just shook his head.

But one day, he showed me how to make a halter for Sky out of just one piece of rope and how to attach another to lead her around with.

I gone out and got it on her all right and tried to lead her around, but Joe kept getting in the way, being right on my shoulder and all. So I got Joe's halter and rope and had him in one hand and Sky in the other.

Well, Sky would head off one direction and tug me that way, or she'd be about to run me over while I was leading Joe with the other hand. Plus the fact that Sky was getting bigger by the day, and harder to handle.

So what I done was to tie Sky's rope onto Joe's tail. He didn't seem to mind that, so then I led Joe up beside the corral fence. With Sky tied on behind him, I climbed up on one of the fence rails and slid onto Joe's back.

At first I thought he might try to buck me off and send us all flying, but he just turned his big head and looked at me sitting up there. I was still holding his lead rope, so I nudged

his sides with my legs and we went around and around that corral, with Sky following behind. And if she tried to go another direction, she couldn't get any farther than the length of Joe's tail.

Uncle Lester didn't see none of this. I don't know what he would have done if he'd spotted us doing that.

Joe's flat, wide back was so comfortable, he was like riding a sofa. Sliding down his side, it was a long way to the ground, but he just stood there waiting for me, and he waited while I untied Sky from his tail. I had to leave Joe in the corral when I taken Sky up to the kitchen door, and that tough old horse just whinnied like a baby.

Then Gramma'd give me the bottle on the kitchen step, and Sky would slurp and chug, and milk would be dribbling out the corners of her mouth. It even brought a smile to Paw Paw's old face sometimes, and that made me happier than anything.

9

SUMMER COME and we got out of
school, and Gramma and I were still
trying to find us a house to live in.
Soon after we moved in with Uncle Lester, I
gone with her to the grocery where she asked
Mr. Barnett if she could sell some of her
bread, and he said yes.

Mr. Barnett's was the second store in
town. It was the place all of us Indians come
to shop.

With him, a customer was a customer. It
was at the other store where they cared what
you looked like.

Well, this day when Gramma brought her
bread in, turned out Mr. Barnett was thinking
of putting in a whole new frozen food section

at the back of his store, but there was this old cabin out back that was in the way. It had been there as far back as anyone could remember.

We could just have it, Mr. Barnett said, but it would cost him fifty dollars to get some guys in with the equipment to move it. And when Mr. Barnett looked Gramma in the eye and said fifty dollars, we knew he needed fifty dollars, and the price wasn't going to go up when you couldn't back out of it anymore. He never tried to cheat Indians. Only thing was, he said, he wanted to get it moved right away so he could start building while the weather was good.

We gone straight home that day and counted out all the money Gramma had saved from selling her bread. Thirty dollars, just about.

We needed twenty more dollars. I figured Uncle Lester was pretty sick of us living in his house by now, so I gone up to him and said we could be moving out any time now, only we were a little short. Just as soon as he come up with twenty dollars, we'd be out of his hair for good.

A couple days later, here he come with the money and given it to Paw Paw and Gramma. I looked real serious on the outside, but inside I was about to split my sides grinning, because we got our fifteen dollars back from Uncle Lester and a little more.

10

T HE DAY the tractor come grinding
up the road, dragging that sorry-
looking old cabin on what looked
like the biggest travois ever made, was about
the happiest day of my life.

On the spot where our old house stood,
the ground was white. It was like the flood
had scrubbed our house right off the land,
scoured down to the rock. We aimed to put
our new house down on the very same spot.

The dust was so thick I couldn't even see
who was driving up our dirt road, and I could
barely make out the house sliding along on
pine poles. Near to the top of our hill, that old
tractor started spinning its big back wheels
and throwing dirt and rocks everywhere. I

thought the windows in that little house would shatter. But Buzz waved his arms real wide and the tractor man stopped.

The house slid back some, and the dust settled some, and pretty soon here come Buzz with his team of horses. He backed them up to stand in front of the tractor.

Never before and never since have I seen horses hitched to a tractor, but Buzz hitched up his two Belgian crosses, the ones with hooves the size of dinner plates. Then he given the reins to the driver. He started up the tractor and Buzz given a yell, yanked off his belt and slapped his horses on the rear. And he kept on yelling and slapping those horses, and that's how our house got to the place it's in.

We had a job cleaning that little house, sweeping out the dust and washing the walls and windows inside and out. Then we had to paint it because it hadn't had a coat of paint in years. Someone once put linoleum tiles in for the floor, but now they were dirty and chipped. So me and Paw Paw pulled them up, and we painted the old wood floorboards underneath, and it looked real nice.

We had one big room with a sink by the front door, and a water pump beside the sink. We had a wood cooking stove, the kind Gramma was used to. We had a kerosene lamp. And we had a bedroom. And Mrs. Yellowrobe sent her two big boys over to dig an outhouse outside the back door – close, but not too close.

We made new markers for my mom and dad and brother's graves.

At first our new house just smelled like paint. But once Gramma got into it and started the wood stove, the house taken on all the cooking smells and wood smells I remembered from our old house.

Curlybear Wagner, the medicine man, held a blessing for it. He brought his drum, and we gone to all four corners of the house and blessed it. Then he said what Paw Paw said when Sky come to us:

The earth is our mother,
and the sky is our father.
We don't know why there's floods
    and things like that,
but we know that our mother and father
    are wise,
because they come from the Great Spirit
who is wisdom,
and so the earth and the sky
also have wisdom.

Then he thanked the Great Spirit for bringing us back to this land, and he played the drum and him and Paw Paw and Gramma sang a song that lasted a long time. And when they were done, there wasn't no sound but the wind blowing.

We didn't have nothing, hardly, to put in the house, but we had a house, and that was something. I kept the picture album at the bottom of my little cardboard box of clothes, and now and then I'd stick my hand down there to where it was lying, just to make sure it was still safe.

We slept on the floor for a long time until we could save up enough money to buy a bed, and Buzz brought us over a table and chairs. He was rebuilding, too. Just like us, when the wall of water come through, it taken Buzz's house clean away, and then the water rolled on past and left the land standing where it was. Well, some people brought Buzz two tables and about six chairs. Buzz said he didn't need so much furniture, so we split them up between us.

Uncle Lester even helped me put up a fence for Sky, and man, that was the hardest thing I ever done. Plus we had to put up a coop for our share of the chickens Lester, Gramma and Paw Paw bought. Lester's idea was to build a lean-to right up next to the house, so the warmth from the house would help keep the chickens from freezing in winter.

We hauled up a couple of tree trunks from down in the gash that Birch Creek trickled in. There was a lot of trash left over from the flood down there. And we turned those tree trunks into posts for the lean-to. We got a big sheet of plywood for the roof. One end of the plywood got nailed into the side of our house, and the other end of the plywood got nailed onto the tree trunk posts. Then we boarded up the sides and left a doorway so the chickens could run in and out.

So when it come time to build a shed for Sky, I said, why don't we do the same thing, right down the side of our house from the chicken coop? Well, Lester turned his head a little like he'd never thought of that. But we done it my way, so I guess it seemed like a good idea to him. We had to go back down by the creek to gather up more flood trees and stuff that we could use. And we had to make it bigger. But I'd been worried that Sky might get lonely at our place without Joe. I figured the chickens could keep her company. And on that side of the house, she'd be out of the wind.

By the time it was all finished I thought my hands never would recover from getting sliced and poked on that barbed wire fencing, and from all the times I pounded my thumb instead of a nail.

Then we went and brought Sky over from Uncle Lester's place, and I thought poor old Joe was gonna try and jump the corral fence to come with us. I reached over the rails and given him a big hug and rubbed his face while Lester just stood there with his mouth hanging open.

We put Sky in her new spot, and Paw Paw come out and looked at the whole thing for the first time. He never come out to help when we built it. It was like it was just too much work for him, and I gone in sometimes and found him asleep in his chair. But when Lester and I dragged Gramma and him out to see all the work we done, he looked real proud of me and stroked my hair. I put my arms around Sky's neck, and she nuzzled me so hard I almost fell over.

I think that was the last time I ever heard Paw Paw laugh.

11

PAW PAW DIED the next winter, during the warm break in January. That was the next time Curlybear come over.

Gramma, Buzz, Uncle Lester and me, and all the Yellowrobes stood between patches of old snow around Paw Paw's grave while Curlybear talked about Paw Paw's life. He told about times even farther back, about the Salois Cree people coming down from Saskatchewan. Cree is our tribe's name. Salois is our family's name.

All us Cree escaped down over the border after the Mounties captured Louis Riel, leader of the Métis. Those were people with French and Indian blood in them. Riel was trying to form an Indian nation up in

Saskatchewan. There was a battle, and the Mounties got Riel and planned to hang him.

We snuck down here with Gabriel Dumont, Riel's right-hand man. He married a Cree woman, and she and Gabriel Dumont were Gramma's grandparents. Somewhere along the way, any of us who spoke French back then dropped speaking French but kept on speaking Cree.

Then Curlybear told how the Blackfeet people took in all of us who settled in this spot. They helped hide Dumont from the U.S. cavalry, who were looking for him because the Mounties wanted to hang him, too. Curlybear named everybody from Dumont through Gramma and Paw Paw's children down to me. He remembered everybody in the family. And he fit in all the people that were there for Paw Paw's funeral.

We buried Paw Paw with the belt buckle he always worn. It didn't seem right for anyone else to wear it.

Gramma didn't say nothing until long

after dark that day. Then she turned to me and said if it wasn't for me and Sky, Paw Paw would have died right after the flood, but we given him reason to live. I hugged Gramma tight after she said that, and we both had a good cry. Then I slept next to her in the bed we'd bought for her and Paw Paw that Christmas. It was our one, big present.

Sky knew all about it. I'd go out and talk to her and brush her and bury my face in her neck, and she'd nuzzle me kind of gentle.

I worried over Gramma after Paw Paw died, because I thought she wasn't the strong one of the family, that Paw Paw was. But I found out maybe she was the strong one after all. We'd lie in bed at night with our arms around each other, her smelling like all the kitchen smells of that day, and she'd tell about her and Paw Paw in the early years.

She told me how, when Paw Paw was nineteen or twenty, he joined up with an Indian regiment to fight in the First World War. They got sent over to France. Paw Paw come back speaking French, and he learned how to fix truck engines, so when he come back he almost always had work fixing people's engines.

12

I MISSED A COUPLE weeks of school when Paw Paw died. In our tradition, when someone dies, it's important to take time out, and not to rush back into things.

The morning I got back to school, our teacher, Mrs. Nail, shown the whole class the list of names of kids who got all A's that report card term. She read out the names. Me and Jenny got straight A's and we knew it because our report cards said so. But our names weren't on the list.

So when the recess bell rung, Jenny and me gone up to Mrs. Nail and asked her why our names weren't on the list.

Mrs. Nail stood right in front of us and looked at us. She looked at the list in her hand.

"Oh, this list. This list is just for white children," she said.

Later that first day I was back, we had a test. I known all the answers to the test, but some of the white girls across the aisle from me written up a cheat sheet with the answers on it. I was in the middle of taking my test when those girls were making noise with that sheet, passing it to each other.

Mrs. Nail looked up to see what was going on, and one of the girls slid that cheat paper onto the floor where it landed right under my feet.

Mrs. Nail got up out of her chair and bent over to pick up the sheet. Then she called me out into the hall.

Standing in the hall with my back pressed against the wall, I told her it wasn't mine. It wasn't even in my handwriting. Besides that, one of the answers was wrong, and I told her.

"Don't you sass back to me, you little–"

She didn't say little what. Mrs. Nail sent me to the principal, who sent me home for the rest of the day, and I got a big fat F on the test.

Walking home, I decided I was quitting school. I wasn't going to put up with those kids who made fun of us until we wanted to punch their lights out. And I wasn't going to put up with a teacher like Mrs. Nail who tried to fail me every chance she got.

It was a long way to walk home from town. I had plenty of time to plan out my speech to Gramma for why I was never going back to school.

I walked in the door. She was sitting at the kitchen table having a cup of coffee. A dozen loaves of fresh bread were cooling on the stove.

I told her everything that happened, and what I planned to do.

"Ain't no way you're quitting school," she said. "As long as you're in that classroom you're going to learn something."

Then she told me about how when she was little, some white people come around and took all the Indian kids to live at one big school. They come to take her away when she was only six years old. Some of the kids got sick and died. From the kids who survived, some were chosen to be in school, but some of the kids were sent to work in the kitchen or clean the rooms, and she had to work instead of go to school. That's how come she never learned to read or write much.

And then Gramma said, "Paw Paw wanted you to go as far in school as you could go. He told me, 'You keep after her. See she uses that head of hers.'"

We sat together at the table, saying nothing for awhile.

Then Gramma said, "Your dad, your mom, they wanted you to go to college, make your people proud. They wanted it for your brother, too. But now you're the only one can make it happen."

I scraped my chair against the floor, got up from the table and walked outside. I buried my face in Sky's thick coat. I held her mane in my fists and smelled her fresh horse smell. I put her halter and lead rope on her, and we gone for a long walk through the windy grass. We stood at the edge of Birch Creek. I stared into the gash while Sky grazed on brown grass between patches of snow.

Next morning I was on the bus to school.

13

ONE SPRING DAY when the grass was turning green again and the air had that spring smell to it, Gramma and me were both thinking about how we used to birth lambs and how they'd be out to grass by now.

That's when we got out the picture album and opened it.

We took all day, Gramma telling me about all the pictures. Toward the back was where I come in, curly-haired and in some frilly dress I don't remember, held by my dad and my mom holding my baby brother. Then all of a sudden there was just me standing outside the old house with the snow way over my head behind me. And next to me was Paw Paw.

Always there was Paw Paw, standing quiet, tall and thin with those braids getting grayer by the page. In my head I could hear the old songs, I could hear a drum beating and the long-ago Cree people with him, singing.

14

I'D PESTERED Paw Paw ever since Sky come to us about when I was gonna get her broke to ride. I asked him when would he teach me, and he just said in about a year. But Paw Paw was gone. In the end, it was Buzz that helped me get Sky broke.

Everybody knew that Buzz was so good with horses he'd even been in movies doing stunts with them, and he gotten Paw Paw work in one movie that was made in Montana. I thought Buzz would get Sky trained in no time.

First thing we done, once spring really taken hold, was to take Sky to Buzz's corral, so she couldn't run off if I tried to get on her. I showed Buzz all the ways I could get her to

turn and follow me when she was in that
rope halter Paw Paw made for me. Buzz
acted pretty impressed, maybe because Sky
had grown into a big horse, and I come up
barely to her withers.

I thought somehow, with Buzz there, I'd
just get on her and she'd be broke. But it
didn't work that way.

I tied her to Buzz's hitching post inside his
corral gate. Buzz lugged a couple saddle pads
out of the barn.

"Now," he began, "if she's gonna get used
to you on her back, start by letting her sniff
one of these. Then we're gonna sack her out."

"Sack her out?"

"We're gonna rub her down with it."

"Rub her down?"

"Yeah. Like this." And Buzz taken the saddle pad and he let her sniff it to get the smell
of it. Then he touched it to her sides, her
back, her chest, even her legs.

That part was pretty easy. She gotten used
to having a blanket on her when we first

found her, and I'd rigged up some straps to keep the blanket on when the nights were cold.

Next Buzz said to jump up on one side of her so I wasn't on her back, just kind of hanging myself off her left side. So I grabbed some of her mane in my left hand and I put my right arm across her back, and I tried to jump up on her like I was gonna mount her. But she was so tall that Buzz had to lift me up so my stomach was flat against her back, and I could hang down her side. She tried to step away from me, but I hung on while she danced around probably thinking what a crazy person I was. She could've tried to rub me off on the fence rails, but she didn't.

Then Buzz said I had to do that on the other side of her, too. He given me a boost. She pretty much stood in one place that time, and when I slid down from her I given her a big hug.

And then I realized something.

Buzz was gone.

He was gone, and he wasn't coming back. It was up to me to train her.

Next thing I done was to try to get on her myself. I seen how Buzz and Paw Paw would grab big tufts of mane in one hand, stand next to the horse facing the horse's tail, then swing their right leg up and swivel right onto the horse's back.

To see them do it, it looked so easy. I'd swing up and hit my leg on Sky's ribs and fall on the ground underneath her. Plus the fact that Sky decided she didn't want to stand still for me. She danced around like a kid who has to go to the bathroom real bad.

I tried it again. Sky was just too big for my legs. I led her up to the fence rails. Then I gone around and climbed up on one of the rails like I done to get on Joe.

I had my feet on one of the rails and my hands on her mane, when all of a sudden she jumped away from me, and I gone plowing into the ground.

I tried to think what I could do next. I pushed her head down and straddled her neck. Then I pulled her head up with the lead rope and slid down her neck onto her back, nice and snug.

Sky turned sideways so fast she left me standing on the ground even before I known what happened.

"She don't want to be rode, Georgia."

I swung around and there stood Buzz, holding his sides laughing.

I didn't find it so funny.

"Well, she's gonna get rode, and I'm gonna be the one to do it," I said. And I pushed her head down again.

I remembered Paw Paw talking about horses having a way of giving up if you're persistent. I straddled her neck again, and when I pulled on the lead rope, she raised her neck. And I fell right off without getting even close to her back.

Sky started to get the idea of what I was trying to do. I pushed her head down and straddled her neck, and I slid down onto her back, and she stood still.

I sat as still as I could. Then I scratched

her neck, told her what a good girl she was. Just like old Joe, she turned her head to look at me sitting up there.

I was real proud that I was up there sitting on her back, and it felt great. Getting her to take a step forward was another story.

She stepped back. She stepped sideways and in a circle, but going forward was going to be a piece of work. I decided I had to get off her and go find another piece of rope to attach under her halter, along with the one I already had on her.

I found a lead rope in Buzz's barn. His horses were all out grazing in their field. I hooked that rope under her chin and then put the two ropes on each side of her neck like reins.

After a couple more tries, I was sitting on her back again. With both ropes I could turn her head easier in whatever direction I wanted her to go. If I turned her head a little and tapped her sides with my feet, she taken a step or two. Whenever she taken even one little step, I patted her neck and rubbed her and said, "Good girl, Sky."

It was a good thing it was late spring and the days were getting long. I'd started her early that morning, and it was getting to be sunset when I rode her out of Buzz's corral toward home that same day, when not even a breeze was blowing through that windy land.

I happened to look back over my shoulder in the direction of Buzz's place, and there he was, standing by the open corral gate, tipping his hat to me.

15

RIDING SKY slowly across the field, I could see our house, first a little speck. Then it got bigger and bigger as we rode up home. From a distance I could see how the flood had changed the land, pulled up trees and washed away dirt in some places, leaving only rock. I could remember what it used to look like.

The sky was turning from blue to gold, lighting up the clouds.

I could see the new dam that was built in the mountains where the old dam busted away. I could see Paw Paw's grave next to the new markers for my mom and dad and brother.

As we got closer to the house, I could see

Gramma sitting on the porch shelling peas. The Yellowrobes had brought over two grocery sacks of peas from their garden. They were up to their ears in peas.

The clouds in the sky were turning from gold to red.

Gramma stood up. I slid down off Sky and stood in front of her. She looked at me like I was somebody different.

Then she spoke.

"My grandmother used to say, anyone who trains up her own horse will know freedom and the respect of others. You can be proud of who you are."

Well, I wished Paw Paw could've seen me at that moment. And my dad, and my mom, and I wished my brother was there so I could teach him what Paw Paw and Buzz and old Joe and Sky had taught me. Teach him how to stay in school even if it seems like everybody's against you.

But Gramma seen me. She known what it meant.

And then I known, too.

That I could do whatever I put my mind to. That sometimes we don't get what we need. But we got each other.

Yep. We got each other.

Author's Note

Sky is a work of fiction based on a historical event.

The spring of 1964 saw record rainfall across the northwestern United States and western Canada. The ground was saturated and dams were full.

Then, at 1:25 p.m. on June 8, 1964, a fierce rainstorm surged over the Rocky Mountains of Montana and Alberta. Dams burst. Every highway or bridge that crossed any of the river valleys in that area was washed away. Fast moving waves of water caught many people with almost no time to evacuate from their homes.

At least twenty-seven people lost their lives in flash floods that June day.

At the top of Birch Creek, near the town

of Dupuyer, Montana, the Swift Dam was completely destroyed.

Just downstream from the Swift Dam, on a ranch along Birch Creek, Georgia Salois Phillips lived with her grandparents. Though she was a young girl at the time, Georgia happened to look out the back window of their cabin just as the dam burst.

Although every building on their ranch was completely washed away, Georgia's quick action saved her grandparents' lives and her own life as well.

I am deeply indebted to Georgia for the stories she has told me about that time, for her wide-ranging knowledge of horses, for her love of the harsh and beautiful Birch Creek landscape, and especially for the great courage she showed as a girl and continues to show throughout her life.

Each year a memorial service is held at the Museum of the Plains Indian in Browning, Montana, to honor all who lost their lives in the catastrophic flood of June 8, 1964.

They will never be forgotten.